Wally the Wooly, Wandering Walrus

Rachel Horton

FOR AVA

The kindest, most loving daughter a mama could hope for.

CONTENTS

	Acknowledgments	i
1	Wally at Home in the Arctic	1
2	Mischief Ensues	Pg 4
3	Wally's Adventure	Pg 10
4	The Kindness of Strangers	Pg 14
5	Wally's Special Raft	Pg 18

ACKNOWLEDGMENTS

Thanks to Justin and Ava for supporting me as I pursue my passion and not getting irritated when I constantly have a laptop in my lap after work and on weekends. Thanks to the real Wally the walrus for inspiring this story. Thanks to ChatGPT for providing a rough draft and structure, and to DALL-E for the beautiful illustrations.

1 WALLY AT HOME IN THE ARCTIC

In a time not long ago, in the frigid waters of the Arctic, there lived a wooly, wandering walrus named Wally.

"EEEEYYYYghhaaawwwww," yawns Wally as he awakens from his morning nap, letting out a long, rumbling vibrato breath as he rolls

onto his side and opens his eyes.

"Phweeee, phweeee, phweeee," whistles Wally's walrus pal, Joachim, as he plants a smooch on his girlfriend, Rosy. "Muuuuaahhh."

Peering out into the distance, Wally spies the glowing pink midnight sun drifting just above the horizon. The painted sky swirls in purples, oranges, pinks and deep blues. The vast and serene landscape comforts Wally's wooly heart - so still and surreal.

Here, he's surrounded by a herd of wooly walruses hauling out across the massive, icy beach.

Wally nuzzles up to his buddy, Joachim.

"Ruff, ruff, ruff," he barks as he playfully taps his pal. The walrus buddies swap friendly pats with their flippers and touch tusks, exchanging butterfly kisses.

They huddle together for warmth, safety, and camaraderie in their shivery Artic home.

Little does Wally know, this is the last time he'll be hanging with his walrus pals for a long, long time.

2 MISCHIEF ENSUES

Friendly as could be, Wally might be the kindest walrus you could meet. But he has one little habit that gets him into all sorts of mischief:

He loves naps!

Sometimes Wally snoozes so long, he forgets where he is.

Blink. Blink. Blink. Blink. Wally's eyes slowly begin to open. He's been sleeping on his cozy iceberg even longer than usual. As his eyes blink open, he is startled to see something he's never seen – it's vibrant, rich, mossy, and bright.

It's the color green.

Wally props up on his flippers to get a closer look.

Where can I be??? He muses to himself as he peers across the strangely curvy, dancing water all around him. He's floating past a tiny island dotted with things he's never seen – they're called trees.

Plop, plop, plop, SPLASH! Wally rolls across his shrinking iceberg into the raging sea.

The water feels so strange – like a thousand tiny pricks of heat all over his wooly walrus skin.

He flips and flops and struggles to get back on his iceberg, which is much smaller than he remembers.

What a strange place this is.

Finally situated back atop his floating icy raft, Wally looks all around. He sees tiny icebergs in almost every direction. They look so different, weirdly shaped with colors he's never seen. Little does he know, these icebergs are not icebergs at all. They're boats!

Am I having a dream? Wally thinks to himself. He taps his eyes with his flippers and blinks and blinks.

Did I nap my way into a whole new world?

He looks around and sees a massive beach not far away. It's a place called Ireland.

Jeepers!

Wally feels stunned. Where are his pals? Just as he starts to worry, Wally hears a rumbling grumble and turns to see a special tiny iceberg moving toward him.

Atop the colorful craft are three funny-looking animals walking on stilts. One of them shouts:

"Helloooo thar!"

These are the strangest creatures Wally has ever seen!

Wally starts to realize he's a very long way from home.

One thousand, five hundred miles is how far he is, in fact.

He's got himself in a pickle.

In fact, he feels emotionally exhausted. This has been a lot to process.

Before he knows it, he's taking another snooze as his iceberg floats across the Celtic Sea.

3 WALLY'S ADVENTURE

Awakened by the heat, Wally rocks the yacht back and forth as his barks echo across the cove. He's been snoozing on the bottom deck of a Spanish businessman's seacraft for hours. His iceberg got too small to hold him, and he had to find another one.

"Saludos!" The man shouts.

You see, Wally weighs 1,700 pounds. That's the same weight as two grand pianos.

"Bwwwhhhhaaaaaaaaaa," Wally bellows as he rolls from his left side to

his right. He plunges into the warm, salty water and goes for a long

swim. He dives down and swallows a few fish. After awhile, he nears a vast sandy beach.

Exhausted, he lets the tide push him closer and closer toward land until he finds himself basking in the sun on a beach in France.

Wally waddles onto the sand and a little girl named Ava approaches.

"Look! It's a walrus!" she exclaims. A small crowd gathers around, excited to see the unusual visitor.

"Bonjour!" says a friendly man with a kind smile. "You must be lost. What's your name?"

"I'm Wally!" he says. "I fell asleep and woke up in a place called Ireland. Then I floated on a weird-looking iceberg to get to this place."

"Hahahaha, hehehehe," the sound of the crowd's laughter makes Wally feel embarrassed.

"That wasn't an iceberg, Wally! That was a boat," Ava says.

"I've seen a lot of those boats," Wally says, "but when I try to climb on

12

board, they flip right over and sink to the bottom of the sea!"

The crowd laughs again, but this time, Wally's eyes well up and a tear runs down his cheek.

"How will I ever get back home?" he worries out loud.

Wally misses the cold, the snow, and all his wonderful walrus friends.

We're going to help — don't you worry!

"We're going to help, Wally — don't you worry!" Ava says.

Wally rolls over onto his wooly back and takes a long snooze.

While he sleeps, his new friends come up with a plan. They're going to build him a special raft to help him get home.

13

4 THE KINDNESS OF STRANGERS

"Walllllyyyyy!" Joachim's voice echoes through the homesick walrus's dream.

"Where are you, Wally?"

"I miss my friend," Wally thinks to himself as he wakes from dreaming to the sound of, "Tap, tap, tap, tap."

It's the sound of a hammer pounding away to work on Wally's new iceberg.

Wally blinks and blinks to open his eyes. And he can hardly believe what he sees.

His new friends are gathered round – they've made an iceberg – also known as a raft – big enough to float him all the way home.

"We know you miss your Arctic pals," says Ava, "And you must be so hot!"

"Hop onto this special raft we built for you," says another of his new friends. "We're going to help you go in the right direction so you can get back home."

"Muah," Wally touches his right flipper to his lips and blows a kiss to his new friends. He hops onto the raft.

"Thank you for everything!" he says. "I'll miss you all!"

As his new iceberg sails north, Wally feels a mix of excitement and sadness. He's loved his adventure, all his new friends, and the strange, warm waters of the Atlantic.

But he also can't wait to be back in the Arctic with his buddy and the vast icy beach and frigid waters.

5 WALLY'S SPECIAL RAFT

Finally, Wally's special raft reaches the Arctic.

It feels so good to be back! Wally is happy to see Joachim and Rosy and gab all about his adventure.

From now on, Wally always makes sure to nap in a safe spot so he won't drift away again. But sometimes, he thinks about his colorful friends in the sunny seaside towns.

And he smiles, knowing that no matter where he goes, friends can be found in the most unexpected places.

And now, all in the world is well – because Wally the wooly, wandering walrus, is *home*.

ABOUT THE AUTHOR

Rachel Horton is a Dallas-based marketing and communications leader who has built and led marketing and communications functions across four different industries over 27 years, having led marketing and communications teams at Texas Health Resources, Texas Instruments, Micron, and SMU Lyle School of Engineering.

Rachel has a degree in Journalism from Pepperdine University. She started her career as a reporter in Dallas, winning an Associated Press Managing Editor's Award for a series of articles for the Arlington Morning News in 2000.

Rachel currently leads a marketing and communications team at SMU. She is also working on a new book and doing some consulting work on the side.